T0209449

— Jacob *and* Faye —
A Grandparents Story

INSPIRED BY TRUE EVENTS

DAPHNE LEIGH

WESTBOW
PRESS®
A DIVISION OF THOMAS NELSON
& ZONDERVAN

This is a work of fiction. All of the characters, names, incidents,
organizations, and dialogue in this novel are either the products
of the author's imagination or are used fictitiously.

WestBow Press books may be ordered through booksellers or by contacting:

WestBow Press
A Division of Thomas Nelson & Zondervan
1663 Liberty Drive
Bloomington, IN 47403
www.westbowpress.com
1 (866) 928-1240

ISBN: 978-1-9736-3506-2 (sc)
ISBN: 978-1-9736-3505-5 (e)

Library of Congress Control Number: 2018908816

Print information available on the last page.

WestBow Press rev. date: 08/06/2018

Contents

Foreword

Upon beginning my third writing project I am endeavoring to branch out into the world of fiction. My first two books, Life Overcomer and Seriously Now, Enough Already are stories of events that have occurred in my life, and how God has helped me to overcome them all. My vision and passion is to create a set of stories based on truth and history, the history of my family. There is rich family history on both the mothers and fathers side of my family and my interest is in telling their stories.

Jacob and Faye are my father's parents. They have a story of faith and love having survived Constantinople, Turkey during World War One. They joined family in Seattle in 1920 and struggled to raise six children as poor immigrants in a poverty ridden area of the city. It was the connection I felt with the Jewish faith my father was raised with which led me to more study of the Old Testament of the Bible, and eventually led me to a deeper trust in Christ at age 21.

Even though these children were raised in poverty, they were raised with a great work ethic and a strong belief in family. Each of these six children had life long marriages and most started their own business and became successful. The love they witnessed between their parents gave them the foundation they needed to succeed.

There is also a Sephardic Jewish background in this family as they left Spain during the Spanish Inquisition. Therefore this story starts in Seville, the Capital City of Andalusia, Spain, where the family journey began. My hope as you read these pages is that you will fall in love with the story, and with this set of grandparents who I never was able to get to know. Their story is all about faith, family, and the strength that only God can give.

Acknowledgements

I want to thank the people in my life for their constant support as I work on this book. Mom, dad, sisters and brothers, your influence in my life has helped to shape me into the person I am today. Christian family, your support and prayers have watched me grow from my first wobbly steps as a new christian at age 21, and have helped and loved me through each experience in life. You have never shied away from speaking hard truths to me and for that I am thankful.

My group of editors from my home group consists mostly of retired school teachers. Gang, this mission would be mission impossible without your help and support.

And for all the others God brings along the way, thank you, thank you and God bless you. It does take a village of committed, faith filled people to complete a project like this. May God bless it and help it to encourage others.

Beloved Homeland

The April, 1483 sun was setting on the city of Seville as Samuel Delgado began his journey home. His day had been long, but productive. Samuel held his head a little higher, his shoulders a little straighter as he thought on the business of the day. He had spoken to three more brick layers and hopes of large orders for the family's brick company made him smile. His family had settled in Seville generations ago and the business of brick making had been passed down from father to son ever since they had arrived. Even before this family of his settled in Seville, they had spent many generations in the rich traditions of the Jewish faith. Samuel loved the special holy days, set apart to remember all the wonders God had done over the centuries. It thrilled his heart to know that from the time this world was created his God was involved with man, and that his Torah had lasted as truth throughout the centuries. He had learned this from his parents, and they had learned it from their parents. Samuel had a total love for God and family, and a total dedication to carrying on the traditions of his faith and his business. Soon he would be passing the torch on to the next generation.

So now the brick business was owned by Samuel, as he was his parents oldest son. He worked hard alongside his brothers Benjamin and Simeon. Together they were known to make the best bricks in town. They had learned from the generations before them the best materials for the perfect consistency, preparing and finally baking the bricks until they were the perfect building materials. He took great pride in the bricks his company produced and it gave him joy to see his materials being used in the city he loved so much. Next year Isaac, his first born son, would turn thirteen years old and be old enough to join him in the family business and learn his trade.

Yes, Samuel decided, this had been a very good day. As he walked down the street that would eventually take him home he led Dolly, his faithful companion and partner in the brick business. He had acquired her as a filly with the name of Dahlia, but to Samuel and his family she was known only as Dolly. She was a strong bay mare with a cream colored mane and tail, She was a hard worker with a willing, compliant spirit. Without Dolly there was no business, nor any bricks. Dolly pulled the wood and steel wagon that Samuel and his brothers had built with their own hands. Their wagon was built for their generation to deliver their own bricks.

This was Samuel's favorite part of the day. He loved to greet the other merchants who were also on their way home and to talk about the business of the day. But his favorite part of this trip home was the conversation he had each night with Dolly. "Dolly" he would say "You are a good friend and a hard worker. You always give me your very best work and you never complain. You are God's gift to our family and a blessing. Without you we would have no business, nor any bricks. I believe you have earned extra grain tonight, my faithful friend. Let's go home and get you rested so you will be strong and willing to work tomorrow." Dolly didn't answer, but the look in her eyes and the new clip in her step told Samuel that she understood. They were going home. She gently nudged Samuel on the shoulder with her nose in a playful manner as they continued on their way.

As they journeyed they stopped to chat with baker Manuel and his wife, and Marcus the coppersmith. They were all part of a good community where people from different backgrounds and different faiths could live together in peace. As they passed by the office of Mr. Sanches the constable, the man appeared in the door and called out to him. "Samuel, may I have a word with you please?" Sanches was the man whom the Spanish government had set in place to be community leader and head officer over the city of Seville.

Samuel nodded, and slowed Dolly to a stop, tying her to the post provided there. Mr. Sanches was a respected man in their community and Samuel's wife, Sarah, visited with this man's wife often. Their children regularly played together in the city streets. Samuel asked "Is there a problem, Sir?" "Please sit down" Sanches said, as Samuel entered into his office.

"As you know, the culture of our city is beginning to change. The Archbishop of Seville believes that this city should be under the authority of King Ferdinando and Isabella of Spain, who are committed to the Church of Rome.

Samuel said, slowly and thoughtfully "I have heard a few rumors of this. Why do you bring the subject up?"

3

The Constable continued, "Samuel, I like you a lot. You are a good man of business and you and your family are important to our local economy. You are respected in your Jewish community, and could hold some influence. If you could work to convert your Jewish friends to the Catholic Church this could all be behind us. Our children play together and our wives enjoy each other's company. I truly want you to stay here in Seville."

"You want us to stay?" Now Samuel was getting agitated, knowing where this conversation was heading.

Sanches stood to his full height and took on an attitude of great authority. "The Archbishop, under the authority of the Pope, has made a decree that the region of Spain is to be under the Holy Church of Rome. I am afraid that there is nothing I can do. If you refuse to convert to the beliefs of the Church of Rome you will have to leave our coasts."

Samuel looked the man in the eye, set his jaw and said, "I am a child of the Most High God. I will offer unto God thanksgiving and pay my vows to the Most High. I will call upon Him in the day of trouble and He will deliver me, and I will glorify Him."

The Constable laughed out loud at this statement. "Now Samuel, be reasonable. There is nothing wrong or bad about Roman beliefs. All you need to do is be baptized in their church and you can stay. You and your family will be fine."

Samuel answered a little louder this time. "I am a child of the Most High God. I will offer unto God thanksgiving and pay my vows to the Most High. I will call upon Him in the day of trouble and He will deliver me, and I will glorify Him."

Mr. Sanches shouted back at him "Don't be a fool!"

Samuel stood. "I am a child of the Most High God. I will offer unto God thanksgiving and pay my vows to the Most High. I will call upon Him in the day of trouble and He will deliver me, and I will glorify Him." And with that, Samuel turned to leave.

"THIS IS NOT OVER" shouted the Constable after him.

Samuel turned and said "Sir, I'm afraid it is".

The Constable's red, distorted face showed the extent of his rage toward Samuel, his family and all who held his beliefs. "You mark my words. The authorities will be sent, your blood may be shed if you refuse to convert and be baptized."

Samuel untied Dolly and resumed his trip home. The street was dark and deserted by now. "Dolly," Samuel said, "Your tender ears should not hear the things my heart feels for that man, for this new society that is taking over. Lord God of Abraham, Isaac and Jacob, I need You like I need my next breath. How could I ever turn my back on You and bow down to Rome? I need You to show me what to do, where to go. Ah, well. Come, Dolly. We must get home. Sarah will be worried." Sarah was the beautiful wife of his youth. This is what he would do. He would go home to his family. After the children were in bed he would talk to his wife about the conversation he had with the constable. She would know what they should do. Together they would work things out.

A Plan Emerges

Dolly's pace quickened as they came in sight of their home. She whinnied her greeting as she saw twelve year old Isaac jog up the path to meet them. He gave her nose a pat as he walked toward the barn with his Father. Isaac looked concerned as they backed Dolly into the special shed they had built for the wagon and unhitched it.

"You were late tonight. Mama was really worried" Isaac said.

"I know, my son. Where are the other children?"

"Mama sent them to do their evening chores. She was holding supper until you came home. Can I help you with Dolly?"

"Always" Samuel answered. Samuel and Isaac worked together to slide the harness and bridle off their horse and led her to her feeding trough. Dolly whinnied and sneezed her thank you as her nose dove into the grain and hay that Isaac had provided for her. "Papa, you work so hard. You need me to help you make and deliver your bricks. Why can't I go to work with you and help you?" Isaac asked.

Samuel smiled to himself, so proud of his young son. "All in God's time, my son. You are twelve years old now. What will happen when you turn thirteen?"

"I will have my bar mitzvah" Isaac answered as he grabbed Dolly's brush and went to work on her coat. He took great pride in the care he and his father took of their partner and friend.

"Yes, that is right. And what will that mean?"

"I will be a man." Isaac held his head a little higher at the thought.

"And then you will be old enough to come to work with me and learn my trade, and help me in my business. Some day this business will be handed down to you and your brothers." Samuel's heart broke for the uncertainty of the future for his son, the beginning of his strength. "Until then, my son, you must study hard and help your mother with the other children. This too brings a blessing."

"Yes, Papa. How is Dolly's leg?" Isaac asked.

Samuel ran his hand down Dolly's leg where she had cut herself on the wagon last week. The horse flinched and stomped her hind foot in response, but continued with her evening meal uninterrupted. "It seems to be healing just fine. Why don't you put some of Mama's healing ointment on it? You finish up with the horse now. I must go inside and make my apologies to your mother."

Isaac chuckled and shook his head. "Good luck with that. She was pretty mad!" He replaced Dolly's brush onto its shelf and went to get Mama's ointment.

Samuel went quietly inside the house, his hat in his hand. As he stepped inside the house Sarah turned from the stew and bread she was trying to keep warm, tears in her eyes. "Samuel, I was so worried!"

"I know, my love. What can I say?" Sarah rushed

to his side and took his face in her hands. He looked so weary, so spent by the work of his day. But there was something else in his eyes that she did not recognize – a deep sadness.

"Something has happened, Samuel. What is wrong?"

"Later, my love. Let me have this night with the family I love. After the children are safely asleep we will talk."

"I will call the children in to dinner." Sarah went outside and clapped her hands loudly. "Children, come wash for dinner. Papa is home now and it's time to eat."

There was great commotion as one at a time, Rebekah, Reuben, Jonathan and Dinah came running in and took their place at the dinner table. Last of all, Isaac, all arms and legs, came rushing in and almost knocked his chair over in the process. This led to a chorus of giggles from the younger children. Samuel watched his young family, savoring the moment. Sarah did her best to hide her amusement.

"Isaac, I did not intend for you to come quite that fast!" By now the giggles had exploded into hilarious laughter.

"Sorry, Mama" Isaac replied as his face turned many shades of red from embarrassment.

"Alright, alright my children" Samuel said. "Let us say a blessing over this lovely meal your mother and sisters have prepared." A new calm came over the dinner table and the family all held hands and bowed their heads as Samuel began to recite their favorite mealtime prayer.

"For all this, Lord our God, we give thanks to you and bless you. May your name be blessed by the mouth of every living being, constantly and forever, as it is written. When you have eaten and are satisfied, you shall bless the Lord your God for the good land which he has given you. Blessed are you, Lord, for the land and for sustenance." They all then dug into the meal that Sarah and her girls had worked together to prepare. Samuel watched his family eat and enjoyed the chatter surrounding him. He could not keep himself from wondering what the future would hold for this little family of his. Many times during the meal he saw Sarah watch his face with a look of concern. Yes, they would deal with this trouble. They would find a way, a place to go where they could serve the God they loved and carry on His traditions without fear.

Later that evening, the children safely asleep in their beds, the time for this important conversation had come. Samuel added wood to the crude wood stove that heated the house and Samuel and Sarah moved chairs closer to the stove to keep their conversation farther away from the children. Sarah spoke first. "Samuel, tell me what has happened. What has made you so sad?"

"Sarah, my dear, you know me too well." Samuel released a heavy sigh and then began his story. "I was on my way home, leading Dolly and the wagon, when I was called into the office of the constable."

"Why, Samuel? What did he say to you?"

"He said that the culture here in Seville is changing. There has been a decree from the Archbishop by authority of King Ferdinando and Isabella of Spain, who are committed to the Church of Rome." Samuel sighed again and a tear escaped and began to make its way down his face. "Sarah, if we do not convert to the beliefs of the

Church of Rome – to be baptized – If we do not turn our backs on all we have come to believe, we will have to leave this country. The Constable made this very clear. Our lives may be in grave danger if we stay. Our God is not welcome here. Seeing this, how can we stay?"

"What? Our families have lived in Seville for generations. What about your business? What of the children? All our friends and our life here?"

"I know, my love. I know. Our life here has been good. God has truly blessed us. But bow down to the Church of Rome? How could we? I'm sorry, Sarah. I can not do this thing!"

Sarah stood and began to pace across the room. "Of course we can not do this. We need to think. We need to make a plan. Where can we go where we will be safe to worship the Lord our God?"

"God brought our fathers safely out of Egypt, and he can show us where to go." This is one thing Samuel had learned, that Jehovah God had always been with him, always led him.

Sarah stopped her pacing in the middle of the room. "Just a minute" she said. She went over to the wood stove and retrieved a box of letters she kept on a shelf above it. She rummaged through the letters until she found what she was looking for. "Here it is. Great Uncle Jacob – you remember him? He was brother to my grandmother… anyway he left Seville years ago and settled with his family in Turkey. This here… this is a letter from my Cousin Arthur. He has taken over Uncle Jacob's mercantile. I guess it's pretty successful. Samuel, we have family in Turkey! Why don't I write him tomorrow and explain the trouble we are in. Here is what we will do. Tomorrow you go and talk to your brothers and make a plan. I will talk to the Rabbi's wife. We can bring with us all the families in our community who can come. Maybe if we can all stay together…"

"All right, Sarah." Samuel chuckled and shook his head. "I knew you would know what to do. God has blessed me with a wise and prudent wife. Tomorrow will be another day. We will make a plan. Our God will help us. He will make a way."

They both walked slowly to the room where the children slept, their arms around each other. Sarah was right. If their community could stay together and find a way of escape they would be alright. Samuel watched Isaac as he slept. He was such a good boy, so strong, such a willing spirit.

"I have always said my son the brick maker. What will become of him?" Samuel thought for a moment. "My son the Merchant? My son the Ship Builder? How about my son the Magistrate?"

Sarah thought on the conversation her husband had just had with the Constable, and what the Magistrates in Seville would soon be doing. "Surely, Samuel, our son can do better than that! Who knows – maybe the country of Turkey will need a good brick maker."

The Journey Begins

Five weeks later the day of their exodus had come. Samuel and Sarah had been diligent in forming their plan of escaping to safety, and had spoken to their family, friends and members of their synagogue, inviting the people to join them on this journey. Sarah had just received word from Cousin Arthur, and he was expecting them. Most of the families they had spoken to accepted the invitation, realizing the situation they would be in if they stayed. There were a few families who had relatives outside their country's borders and they had slipped quietly away in the night and were gone without causing any distraction. This was not Samuel's plan. In conversation with Rabbi Mosher and the rest of their group it was decided that they would not steal away in the night like wounded animals. They were strong people of God with strong convictions and an even stronger faith. Their little convoy would wind through the main street of town in the middle of the business day for all to see. They would make a bold statement that they could not live in a country which would force them to deny their God.

The first wagon of the convoy was driven by Rabbi Mosher and his little family. Everything they really needed was in the back of their wagon, leaving the rest of their possessions behind to be looted by whoever came along. This was a decision each family had made, only talking along what they really needed, allowing each child one favorite toy to bring with them. After the Rabbi's family came the Roan's, and then the Manuel's. Family after family approached the town center. Samuel's brothers, Benjamin and his family, and then Simeon and his family came near the end of the line. Then finally Samuel and his family were at the very end, the beautiful and proud Dolly pulling their wagon. Samuel had decided that he should be the last one out to ensure the safety of the entire group. Sarah sat beside her husband in the front with little four year old Dinah on her lap and six year old Jonathan between his parents. In the bed of the wagon, along with only the possessions they really needed were the other three children. Seven year old Reuben, ten year old Rebekah and twelve year old Isaac, were sitting tall and proud, Isaac with a protective arm around his little sister.

Jonathan looked at his Papa as they approached town. "Papa, where are we going"?

Samuel answered "We are going to a new and beautiful land, and a new life where we can worship our Jehovah God in peace and safety."

"And," Sarah added, "A land filled with plenty of cousins for you to play with." Jonathan looked wide-eyed at his mother, than his face broke into an enormous grin. "That sounds like fun!"

As the end of the wagons approached the town center the atmosphere around them began to change. The family began to hear shouts of taunting from the towns people, words of cursing and distain toward their God. Isaac spoke first. "Papa, make them stop!" Samuel, his eyes straight ahead, squared his shoulders and drove on. "It will be alright, my son." The closer they came to the commotion, the more shocked the children in the back of the wagon became. The entire town of Seville had gathered – not to bid them goodbye, but to taunt them and to speak curses on them and on their God. It was almost more than they could bear. These were people that they knew, respected members of their community. The children with whom they used to play were cursing at them, throwing stones at them and spitting at them. Young Reuben tried to stay strong for his sister, but soon a rebel tear slid from his eye and down his cheek. Rebekah's eyes filled with tears as she cried out "Why, Papa? Why are they doing this to us?" Rebekah buried her face into Isaac's shoulder and began to sob. There were tears in Reuben's eyes as well, but not in Isaac's. What was evident in Isaac's eyes was not tears, but anger.

As they made their way through the town and the chaos, they passed the Constable Sanches' office and saw him and his wife standing in the doorway. Samuel gave him a respectful nod, and the Constable returned the nod. Samuel understood the man's position – he and his family would have been in great trouble if he did not carry out the decree. By now, Sarah's face had turned ashen white. This city had been their home for generations. She had never seen this behavior from these people she had lived around so long. She turned to her husband. "Samuel, what if we had not made it out? What would have become of our family and our friends?" Samuel nodded. "I believe our friend the Constable did us a great favor, warning us that this was coming."

The person who was having the hardest time dealing with this difficult scene was young Isaac. All he knew is that these children who had recently been his good friends were now his enemies. Five weeks earlier, Isaac's future had been secure. He was prepared to join his father's business in the next year. And then he would be groomed to take the business over some day and run it himself. Now he was on his way who knows were, to do who knows what. And he was very angry indeed.

Samuel, looking at his son from the front of the wagon was not happy with the rage he saw in Isaac's eyes. As they left the mayhem of the city center he spoke. "Isaac, take a good look at our Dolly. How do you think she feels about all of this?" As Isaac watched their horse his eyes were opened. Faithful, beautiful Dolly seemed undaunted by all the taunting. She just kept moving ahead at a good pace, eyes straight ahead, ears pitched forward. Her tail swished back and forth as if she didn't have a care in the world. Isaac learned a valuable lesson from the horse he loved, and he got the message loud and clear. "Papa, I think that Dolly is the smartest horse in the world! Our family is together. We are safe and we are heading to a new land where we can serve our God." Isaac turned to his sister, Rebekah. "God has truly blessed us in Seville." He jerked his thumb towards the mayhem that they left behind them. "Our God can not bless that! Anywhere would be better than living there now."

Rebekah nodded and began to wipe her tears away. Samuel turned and looked at his son with pride. "Well said, my Son. God of Abraham, Isaac and Jacob go before us and prepare the way. Make our journey safe and bless us in the land of Cousin Arthur." With that the entire family looked to the wagons before them, and to their God who would protect them and prosper them in this new and mysterious land of Turkey.

Jacob's Joy

1915 Constantinople

Jacob Romano was in love. All who knew him, all who had ever known him knew this. It was evident by the vibrant light in his enormous brown eyes and the smile that was forever on his lips. His beloved Faye, or Fanny as she was called by those who knew and loved her, had been part of his life as long as he could remember. Their families had been close friends for generations. They had escaped Spain as a community when the Spanish Inquisition occurred and Jacob's ancestor, Samuel Delgado had worked with Faye's family to begin a large ship building business. Their location was where the Aegean Sea and the Black Sea meet and empty into the Mediterranean Sea. This was a great asset to their business and their families had worked well together. There was a great respect for both families in their community as they both shared a strong love for God, for their families, and for the traditions of their Jewish faith. Jacob and Faye had been close friends all their lives and Jacob had always been her strongest protector, being three years older than her. He knew that he wanted to marry her from the tender age of ten years old. It took Faye a little longer. She did not confess her love for Jacob until she was twelve. Their love now confessed, their families informed, there was nothing more to do but to wait until they were grown and old enough to marry. It was the perfect match given the family's generations of working together.

The marriage was in preparation as Jacob was reaching age eighteen. Even though Faye was still young, their families had witnessed their strong love for each other for many years, and Faye's family gave their permission to Jacob to ask for her hand in marriage. In 1914 there was only one thing that could interrupt their perfect lives and postpone this upcoming marriage, and that thing was war. The Turkish Regime at that time sided with the Central Powers of Germany and Austria-Hungary. It seemed like an impossible reality but the Ottoman Empire, which their families had been devoted to and committed to, began an attack against Armenian Christians who had called Turkey their home for generations. This turn of events left the Armenian families, and their entire communities in grave danger. Jacob and his family, and others in the Jewish community worked together in secret to build ingenious hiding places in their homes to hide some of their Armenian friends from the Ottoman Army. The families would then help the Armenians find a way of escape from danger. Some of these hiding places worked, some did not. So much blood was shed. So many Armenians were removed from their homes to what Jacob knew would be torture and sure death. How could his beautiful, faithful Constantinople make such a tragic error? Could they not see the insanity of their own Government? No powerful or failing Government was worth this tragic loss of life. Fortunately, Jacob and his family were able to build a cellar beneath their house which had a seamless trap door, and therefore went undetected by the military forces who would come to investigate, and possibly turn them over to the Ottoman authorities. Nobody knew about this cellar but the Jacob and Faye's family. This cellar had a supply of food and water and was always stocked with enough supplies to last them a week. Jacob lost count of how many times Faye and her family had rushed over to their home with word that the authorities were coming. Both families would take refuge in this secret cellar, and Faye would sit next to her Jacob, her face buried in his shoulder. She was so very young, still a school girl in reality, yet she loved him and trusted him completely. Many times Jacob had lost himself in her eyes and reassured her that this great God that they served had brought the children of Israel safely out of slavery in Egypt. He had also brought both their families safely out of Spain and led them to their new country. This God was big enough to keep them safe during this time of war.

It was decided that their marriage needed to wait until the war was over, or until they found their way out of danger. So the wedding plans were put off for a few more years, but their love for each other remained stronger than ever. Their plans for marriage and raising a family were stronger than any war. Even this war. Their Jehovah God would get them through this and keep them safe. He would help them to use this time of grave danger and fear for their lives to grow them up and to make them stronger. On the days when Jacob was not in danger he worked with his father in his business, and they tried hard to stay out from under the radar of the authorities. Jacob was a hard worker and saved all the money he could so that he could provide for the future of his young bride. Finally after four years of great hardship and peril the war was over, and a new challenge presented itself. With Germany and its Allies losing the war, Jacob's city was occupied by French, British and Italian Forces to keep the peace and to enact the Armistice of Mudros. Jacob and Faye and their families were safer now and no longer in hiding, and again they could proceed to plan their life together. Now, with this new occupation of foreign troops there was talk beginning about a rebellion, and resurgence of the Turkish Army. Jacob was compelled by this group to join their ranks and attend meetings which involved formulating a plan for the future of the Turkish Army. He reluctantly agreed to become part of the rebellion but also had grave concerns. How could he trust this new army when the previous one had put his Armenian friends in such grave danger and shed so much innocent blood? But Jacob also felt the upcoming rebellion would be a tool for his country to put their tragic past behind them and move on with a show of great strength. This was why Jacob agreed to get involved with this group, along with his best friend, Sam.

It was at one of these meetings that Jacob and Sam had some time to actually talk. "Two more weeks, Jacob. How is the ceremony coming together?"

Jacob turned to him with twinkling eyes and a cheesy grin. "I know." said Sam. "You don't have to tell me again. Fanny is the light of your life. She can cook like my grandmother, sing like an angel and has the faith of Sarah, Rebekah and Deborah put together."

"That about says it. Now to answer your question, the plans are coming together fine. Fanny has been busy sewing, cooking and planning for the big day. You are still standing up with me?" Jacob asked.

"I wouldn't miss it. Really, Jacob, I'm so happy for you. Sure, I've endured twelve years of silly talk about your girl." Sam made a funny face. "I pray that some day God can bless me with this kind of love."

Jacob answered "He will, my friend. He will." Jacob smiled at Sam and slapped him on the back. Then the other young patriots arrived for the meeting and the conversation turned to plans for the revolution.

Jacob's Calling

The wedding was wonderful and Jacob was so very happy. He was spending more time and effort with the revolutionary group and had been offered an officer's position in the new Army. Even with Jacob's reservations on where these plans were going he accepted. If he was anything he was a patriot, and willing to fight for the freedom of the country he loved. He was also committed to finding a way to provide a safe and stable home for his new wife where they could raise their children – a whole house full. Days after their wedding, Faye's father moved her family to London, England to pursue business opportunities with a friend there. He had seen enough of war and occupation and was ready to start over in a new environment. Faye moved in with Jacob and his Parents to begin their new lives. The last eight years in Constantinople had been so difficult, so much blood had been shed. Jacob knew he needed to keep his options open as well.

He had just heard from his brother, Isaac. Isaac had been named after the son of their ancestor, Samuel Delgado, who had brought safe passage to their little community from Spain in the early 1480's and he had proudly shared the story with his children, and grandchildren. These grandchildren kept the tale alive and shared it with his grandfather and his father. Like this Isaac, Jacob's brother Isaac was the oldest, the beginning of his father's strength. His brother took great pride in carrying on the ancestral name. And in the same spirit of adventure he set off for America one week after Jacob and Faye were married. There had been ships passage for Isaac, his wife Elizabeth and their two children to New York, then train tickets purchased which took them all the way to the West Coast, to the city of Seattle. Isaac's letter detailed the adventure they had undergone and let Jacob and his family know that they had arrived safely at their destination. He had found a small house to rent and hoped to purchase it someday. "This truly must have been an adventure, my brother," Jacob said as he finished reading the letter. This may be an option, if this revolutionary group became too dangerous. His country had turned their back on his family because of his Jewish faith before. It could happen again. He met up with Sam on the way to another revolutionary meeting.

"Sam, how is your family?" Jacob asked as he vigorously shook hands with him.

"Not as well as yours I can see!" He elbowed Jacob in the ribs as he winked at him. "You will need a larger uniform soon when we begin to take back our country if Fanny doesn't stop cooking such good food. I guess there is something to be said about staying single."

Jacob laughed. "I know, my friend, I know! My wife is a fabulous cook and is determined to make me fat! So, I have been meaning to talk to you about the future of this group of ours. How do we continue to make this revolution work alongside our faith in our Jehovah God? I've been worried about this, Sam. Our country has turned its back on our faith before. It could happen again."

"What has faith to do with our revolution?" Sam asked. Sam had begun to question things during the previous war. He was not as strong in his faith as Jacob, and in many ways had continued with the local synagogue to make his parents happy. He did not have the living, vibrant faith of his parents or Jacob and his family. It seemed lately like the revolution had become Sam's new faith. "I really don't see what being a Jew has to do with being involved in the revolution!" Sam sighed, clearly frustrated. "Look, Jacob. I am not like you. I don't have a wife to be concerned about. With this revolutionary army we are building it's like I finally have something to live for after all the years of war. It's like my life has purpose now. I'm a patriot, and so are you. If our revolution is in conflict with our faith than so be it."

"You truly don't mean that, my friend" Jacob said, looking truly concerned for his best friend.

"I'm afraid I do" Sam said with a determined look in his eye and a set in his jaw. "Now if you'll excuse me, I have a meeting to get to. Our army is about ready for launch and we have plans to make." At that, Sam turned from him and walked briskly away towards their meeting. Jacob could not believe his ears. He had known Sam all his life. He knew that lately Sam had been struggling with his faith, but had no clue that this revolution had taken such a strong hold on him. Jacob made a mental note to guard his own heart against this attitude of supporting his country no matter what. He could not go against what he truly believed. Jacob also decided it was time to write to his brother Isaac to see if there was room for him and Fanny in America if things got really bad here in Constantinople.

Escape to America

Faye finished peeling potatoes for supper that evening, sectioned them and put them into a pot of water to go on the stove to boil. She glanced over at Mama Romano and smiled at her as she cut up pieces of chicken to put in the oven. After they were done there would be gravy to make, bread to warm in the oven and a salad to prepare. All these things combined made up Jacob's favorite meal. Mama was so eager to please her son and Faye loved her for it. She missed her parents and her sister so much after they left for London, but Mama Romano made her feel happy and secure, welcoming her into the family with open arms. Faye knew that she was still very young to take on the responsibility of a husband and running a household. Mama was a wonderful mentor in this area. She had a way of guiding Faye in the best and most economical way to run a home, and at the same time making her feel loved and secure. Mama was also a great mentor in how to make the Jewish holidays and the food shared during these holy times into lifelong memories of their faith and how to make it all into teachable moments. And then there was this new little life growing inside her. Faye found out today that she and Jacob were expecting their first child. Her plan was to break this exciting news to

Jacob and his Parents that night after supper. The chicken done and the bread in the oven, Faye began to work on putting the salad together while mama added flour to the chicken drippings to get the gravy started. Faye looked up from the salad makings and smiled as her husband walked through the front door of their home. What a handsome vision he was in his green Turkish Army uniform. "Hey, you're home early! Dinner will be a little while yet."

Jacob came over and kissed the top of her head, giving her a side hug. But his face looked troubled. "Where is Father? We need to talk." Mama looked up from her work and glanced quickly at Faye. "He's in his study." Jacob kissed Mama's cheek and his eyes twinkled at her. He stole a peeled carrot from Faye's salad makings and she playfully slapped his hand. "Thanks!" he said as he strode toward the study.

Faye gave Mama a concerned look. "Something's wrong." She knew her husband well – the only person on the face of the earth who knew him better was his mother. Mama gave Faye a knowing smile. "You go. Find out what has happened." She gave Mama a kiss on the cheek and turned to follow Jacob into the study. As she left, she spun back around to Mama and said "I'll be back." Jacob had taken a chair opposite Father in the study as Faye arrived in the doorway. "What's up?" she asked. Jacob lowered his head into his hands and Father shook his head. "It's not good" he said. "This revolution is about to take a violent turn." Jacob stood to face his new wife. "Fanny, my sweet Fanny, I can not lie to you. I can't do this. I thought...I thought that this revolution would be a good thing...that it would help our country to move forward after the war. But all I can see now is war. So many years of war. Father is right, this revolution is about to turn very violent. All ethics behind it have gone, and nothing is left but bloodshed." Jacob sighed and shook his head. "As a man, as a Jew who loves God, life and his family, I can't continue to support the revolution."

All Faye felt at that moment was love for her husband and pride in his character. She fell into his arms and rested against his chest, gaining strength from his faithful stance and gaining resolve through the traditions of their faith. Father left them alone to have this moment together. When he returned to the study Jacob shared the most shocking news of all. "There's more" he said. "Sam has turned his back on our God and our faith. Actually the revolution has now become his faith. He sees me now as a traitor and will stop at nothing to force me to continue with my obligations to this ungodly military conflict." Faye shook her head. "Jacob, I'm so sorry. Do whatever you need to do. If we need to go somewhere…away from this new danger, anywhere you are I want to be."

At this moment there was a knock at the door. Mama went to see who it was and returned to the study to announce that Sam was outside. Father sprang immediately into action. "Jacob, to the cellar – NOW!" Mama and Faye lifted up the dining room rug to reveal the seamless trap door to the safe room in the cellar. As Jacob disappeared into the safe room Mama and Faye replaced the rug and put a chair over it. Father approached the front door but Faye stopped him. She gave him a knowing look and said "I'll handle this." She knew Sam well and felt she knew the best approach to take with him.

Faye opened the front door and put on her best smile. "Sam, this is an unexpected surprise! How are you?" Sam briskly pushed her aside and proceeded to search the entire house. Father stepped forward and grabbed Sam by the arm. "What is this about?" he asked, struggling to keep his temper in check. "You come into our house and proceed to search our home like we are common criminals!" Sam stood tall and proud. He took great satisfaction in his new promotion in the revolutionary army. "Sir, I apologize for any intrusion. Jacob left our meeting early today. We of the revolution are concerned that he may defect to Britain as his wife's family has done. The revolution is in need of Jacob's expertise in surveillance and with his knowledge of foreign languages he is invaluable to us."

Faye stepped forward and intercepted the conversation. "I'm sorry, Sam. My husband is not home yet. As to him leaving the meeting early or where he went I have no knowledge." She set her jaw and stood to her full height as she continued. "Jacob is a patriot as are you. Believe me, I will get to the bottom of this. I will speak with my husband." Sam gave Father a salute, and turned his attention to Faye. "And when you do talk to him, let him know that there will be officers coming tomorrow to get him. There will be no more missed meetings." "I understand" Faye said as she walked Sam to the door and saw him out. As she shut the door behind him, she leaned against it for strength. She had taken care of this situation today...but what of tomorrow? Tears filled her eyes as she thought of her sweet Jacob being forced to join a violent military serge he wanted nothing to do with.

By now Mama and Father were in the dining area,

moving the chairs and carpet out of the way and opening the trap door. Jacob emerged, visibly shaken, but so very proud of his young wife. Faye literally flew into his arms. "Jacob, what will we do? They will be back for you tomorrow!" Jacob held her tight until her fears subsided. Then he pulled away and the mischievous twinkle in his eye returned. "I have a plan" he announced. "Before mister Sam so rudely interrupted me I was about to tell you where I went when I left the meeting today. I've been in touch with Brother Isaac and he is part of this plan." Jacob took a deep breath and patted his breast pocket. "I went to the train station and then to the shipyard and purchased two passages on the next voyage to America. We leave tonight."

Faye reeled at the news. America? She had lived in Constantinople all her life and the long trip to America would certainly be challenging, especially now with a baby on the way. But if the previous seven years had taught her anything it taught her that she did not want this new baby to be a child of war. "Jacob, I will come with you under one condition" she said. Jacob looked into her eyes and raised his eyebrows, clearly amused. "And, my love, what would that condition be?" Faye smiled into his eyes and answered. "The condition is this. Brother Isaac must have enough room in his home for three instead of two." Jacob's look of amusement suddenly became one of wonder. His mouth hung open as he stared at his wife. Mama burst into laughter and said "My dear Fanny, I believe you have rendered my son speechless!" Faye winked at Mama and said "This is indeed a first. Yes, dear Jacob. There is a baby on the way. And we will proudly be able to call this child an American.

Mama busily returned to the kitchen and began to dish up their supper. "Ok...A trip to America and a new baby on the way. But my supper is first. The food is going to get cold. Come, Father, Bless this food and our children before they sail into tomorrow."

Jacob held up a hand and stopped the procession to the kitchen. "Wait, there is one more thing." He put both hands on Faye's shoulders and looked into her eyes. "I mentioned the train station as well. We leave tonight on the train...for London. We will have two days to spend with your family before we sail for America on the S.S. Cedric. You will be able to see them before we sail away and tell them of this new child."

Now it was Faye's turn to be speechless. Tears in her eyes, all she could do was to mouth the words "thank you!" The family gathered around the table and stood, holding hands with bowed heads. Father began "Ba-ruch a-tah Adonai Eloheinu Melech Haolam hamotzi lechem min haaretz. Blessed are you, HaShem, our God, King of the Universe, who brings forth bread from the earth. Y'shi-meich E-lo-him k'Ef-ra-yim, v'chi-Me-na she. My son, may God make you like Ephraim and Manessa. O Lord God of Abraham, Isaac and Jacob, go before these children of ours and keep them safe. Though we are devastated to see them go, we understand and know that they will go to a safe place and that Isaac will look after them. Now bless this meal and this, our last evening together." The family sat together and talked amongst each other, eating what they could. Somehow, though, their appetites had left them – with thinking of what would soon happen with Jacob and Faye.

The Voyage

Jacob and Faye stood on the deck of the S. S. Cedric as it approached New York Harbor. This was a special day for them, their first Anniversary. Faye reflected on the events of the past weeks and her heart was filled with emotion. Who would have believed one year ago as they stood in front of their Rabbi and confessed a lifetime of love for each other that their lives would take such an adventurous turn. There were sad good byes which had been said. Mama and Father had taken them to the train station and Jacob and Faye had each packed one suitcase. Jacob had tearfully looked into the eyes of his parents and told them that he would send for them after he had established himself in America. They had indeed spent two wonderful days in London with Faye's family and rejoiced with them about the new baby – her parents first grandchild. Faye's family escorted them to the vessel which would be the next step on this adventure. Again, there were promises to write, and a promise that the family would be sent for when they were settled. But would their families be able to come? The reality of their situation was that only God knew if they would ever see their families again. And in truth, both Jacob and Faye would never be able to see either of their parents again this side of heaven. The other passengers on the Vessel were making their way on deck to witness their approach into the Harbor. The majority of the passengers on the Cedric were affluent families returning from a European vacation. Jacob with the persistence of a desperate man, had been able to book passage from London to New York before they left Turkey. He was committed to looking after his young family.

As the vessel approached Ellis Island, the Statue of Liberty came into view. To most of the passengers this was a sign of coming home. But to Jacob and Faye it was something much greater. It was a sign of freedom and their future. Never again would war ravage their lives. The young couple stood side by side, arms around each other as the vessel docked in their new country. As they disembarked and went through the customs department and registration, Faye looked to Jacob and said, "Ok, what's next?" There were still many challenges to overcome. First was the language of their new home. Jacob and Faye spoke Spanish, the language of their homeland. They spoke very little English. How in the world were they to travel all the way across the country speaking only broken English?

Jacob smiled at her. "Now, to the train station". As they walked the streets of New York they were taken with the size and magnificence of this big city. Jacob walked up to an officer on the street corner and asked him in very broken English where the train station was. The officer pointed them in the right direction. They entered the train station and waited in line for their turn. Jacob did his best to communicate his need for train tickets to the

West Coast. Finally, the ticked agent held up his hand and shook his head. Then he looked over his shoulder and shouted, "Hey, Garcia, over here. Maybe you can understand what this guy needs." Mr. Garcia came over and began speaking to them in Spanish. Jacob smiled, relieved. He silently thanked God for providing a ticket agent who spoke his language. Mr. Garcia produced for them an envelope with enough train tickets to get them where they needed to go. Jacob smiled in gratitude and shook the man's hand. "You should be fine now" Mr. Garcia said. "Just show each ticket attendant the next ticket in your packet and they will show you where to go." Jacob thanked the man and led his bride to a nearby bench to wait for their first train. "Only God could have orchestrated that! We really need to work on our English if we want to be established in America." Faye nodded. Just one more challenge facing their future. But when she thought about all they had survived in their young lives, learning a new language wasn't so hard.

Faye lifted her eyes to Jacob's and held his gaze. "So, have you thought about what you want to do for a job? We know that Isaac is waiting for us at the end of our journey, but you will need to find work. I can help too, Jacob." Faye sat up a little straighter and gathered her courage. "You know that I can cook." Jacob smiled and patted his stomach. "Yes, my dear. Apparently you can cook very well." Faye's cheeks took on a rosy glow at his compliment. "Seriously. I can cook for people. I can wash clothes and iron for our friends and neighbors to help us get by."

"Alright, enough talk. Your hands will be full when

this baby is born. I am young and ambitious. God will be with us and he will help us. If the God of Moses can keep us safe during the war, and bring us safely to America he can surely help me find a good job." Faye sighed. "Alright, Jacob. But remember that I am young and ambitious as well. We are partners and we are in this together."

Jacob checked the train schedule and realized that their first train was about to arrive. "Here we go!" he said. "Now here is what we will do. During our journey we will keep our eyes and ears open. Let's learn all we can about the English language and American culture. We can make it into a little game. It will help us both be ready when we reach our destination." Faye giggled at the idea. "Yes, it can be fun!" So began a one week train adventure which took them across their new country, and it was an adventure indeed. They saw more of the United States than most people who had lived there all their lives. They changed to another rail line in Milwaukee, Wisconsin which would take them west across the Rocky Mountains and to the Cascade Mountain Range. Then it was a short trip to Seattle. They thanked the porter in their best English as they stepped off the train and collected their luggage. They looked around with interest at the activity and noise of their new city. And then suddenly there he was. Brother Isaac had come to meet their train with tears in his eyes. Jacob ran to embrace his brother and they hugged each other and cried for quite a while. Then Isaac turned to Faye.

"This can not be the same girl my brother married. You look like you have grown up into a lovely woman, and a mother apparently." The three of them burst into

A Home and a Family

Two Years Later

Faye worked about her home and began preparations for tonight's dinner. Tonight would be a special night for her and her family. Brother Isaac and his family were coming over for supper and bringing with them cousins who were just arriving from the Old Country. Faye thought often about all the loved ones she and Jacob had left behind when they set off for America. She missed her parents and in-laws so much – family bonds that had formed over a lifetime. But she was excited to see Cousin Alexander and his brother. Alex was to bring one of his twin boys, the other boy would come in about two weeks with his Uncle. She checked quickly on two year old Lucy who was napping in the next room along with Baby Emma. Satisfied that they were safe and sleeping peacefully, Faye went back about her work. She and Jacob had been through a lot of change since they arrived in Seattle two years earlier. Isaac had a dry cleaning business and even though he would have loved for Jacob to come work for him he simply could not afford to hire him full time. Her mind went back to the day, two years earlier, when God had provided Jacob with a job. Faye remembered the day clearly when the husband she was devoted to and believed in announced, two weeks after moving to Seattle, that he was going out to find work. He promised he would not return back home without a job. Faye had prayed for him all that morning. The winter had been cold, and she knew that this would not be an easy task for him. She also knew that her Jacob was a man of his word. He would not return home until he had found employment of some type and she did not expect him home until late.

Jacob had spent the entire morning walking the streets of the business section of downtown Seattle. Any business which was open he would walk inside, introduce himself in his broken English, and ask if they were hiring. He was willing to do just about anything, starting at the bottom and to work hard to succeed. After all, he had a young wife at home with a baby on the way. He was determined to find a way to support his family. "Please, Lord God, help me! There must be someone somewhere here in this city who would be willing to give me a chance. Please, Lord God, guide my steps. Prepare the way before me. It says in the Psalms that your word is a lamp to my feet and a light to my path." Jacob was not accustomed feeling God's calling, but he had a strong impression in his heart right then that God was with him, and not to be discouraged. God had a plan for him. If he followed His commandments he would be a blessing, and his wife and children as well. Jacob suddenly was filled with emotion and thankfulness. "Lord God, I hear you. Give me strength and guide my steps. I need work." He tried a few more businesses to no avail. He was just passing by the Ben Paris Restaurant on 4th and Pine when he decided to stop inside to warm up again and maybe order a cup of coffee.

As the man behind the lunch counter poured his coffee for him, Jacob breathed a silent prayer to heaven. "Excuse me, Sir. My English is not so good. I was wondering if you know where I could find a job. I'm young and strong, and willing to work hard." The man behind the counter thought for a moment, then shook his head. "Sorry, buddy. Jobs are hard to come by in this area. I just had to fire someone because I didn't have enough work for the man." Jacob smiled and said "Thank you. I have been looking for work all morning. I have a wife at home and a baby on the way. I just want to support my family."

There was a businessman sitting next to him at the counter eating lunch. He looked at Jacob with compassion in his eyes. "Ok, Mister. I will pay you ten cents to shine my shoes." Jacob's eyes lit up as the man behind the counter threw him a clean towel. "Yes, Sir!" Jacob replied and quickly went to work on the businessman's shoes. After all, ten cents was ten cents. He shined, and shined until he could see his reflection in the man's shoes. The man inspected his shoes with respect for a job well done. "These shoes are two years old, but you have made them look new. No, better than new. You come back here tomorrow morning at seven o'clock and I'll be here with a friend." Jacob beamed back at him. "Yes Sir!" He then looked back at the man behind the counter. "Thank you," he said as he offered him back his towel.

The man took his towel back and nodded to him. "Now look here, buddy. I'm a family man too. That took courage, what you just did. I'll talk to the boss tonight. This place has needed a good shoeshine for a long time. We can set up two chairs for you by the entrance. It'll be good for business. You work hard like you did today and I'll throw in lunch for you. Be here at seven o'clock tomorrow morning when we open."

Jacob could hardly believe his ears. Him working as a shoe shine? He had never considered such an occupation but this is where the opportunity was. Even a chance for him to start his own business. But he had heard the voice of God, and God had led him there. What would Faye think of him – from businessman and soldier in Constantinople to shoe shine in America? Jacob thanked the man again and promised to return the next morning when the restaurant opened. He then returned home, hat in his hand. He had done what he said he would do. He had not returned home without a job.

Faye had looked up with surprise as he walked through the door. "Jacob, I wasn't expecting you until late. What are you doing here so soon? Something has happened. Tell me what happened!" Jacob could only look at her with a sheepish expression on his face. Finally he took her hand and said "Come, sit with me." They walked together to the sofa in Isaac's sitting room and Jacob took a deep breath. "So, I promised you that I would not return home without finding work. I met a man at a restaurant in the city. And he offered me ten cents to shine his shoes. Apparently he liked what I did. He said that if I came back tomorrow he would bring a friend to get his shoes shined."

Faye looked at the sparkle in his eyes and felt a

little bewildered. Her Jacob shining men's shoes? Jacob continued to tell her about his morning. "I had been out all morning looking for work. I was so cold and so discouraged. So I prayed for the Lord God to help me, to guide me to the right place. To find a way to support you and the baby. And, sweet Fanny, I actually heard God calling me, encouraging me. He said that he was with me, that he would bless us and our children! So a little while later I walked into a restaurant for a cup of coffee and to warm up, and that is where I met this man. The cook there said that if I come back tomorrow morning that he would have two chairs set up for me – that it would be good for business…"

"Ok, Jacob. Slow down! You actually heard the calling of God today? That He would bless us and our children?"

"Yes. Apparently he wants us to have more than one! The cook also said that if I worked hard than he would throw lunch into the deal. But do you think you could respect a husband who shined shoes for a living?"

Faye looked at his sweet face, tears in her eyes. "Jacob, I would follow you anywhere. It doesn't matter to me what you will do for a living. That would not change the man that you are."

Jacob had returned to Ben Paris the following morning, and the head cook there had been true to his word. There were two chairs set up just inside the door and a fresh set of towels for Jacob to use. Before long the man from yesterday returned to the restaurant looking for him with two other businessmen in tow. Thus began Jacob's business as a shoe shine. He worked hard and after his first week lunch was added into the deal and Jacob began to build up a clientele. He always offered them his contagious smile and enthusiasm, encouraging all who he came into contact with at the restaurant, and yes, it was very good for business. The next summer just before Lucy was born, Isaac helped them find a little house on Eighteenth Street in their Capitol Hill neighborhood which was for rent. The landlord was a good, fair man who said that if they were good tenants that someday he might consider selling the house to them.

Her mind returning to the present, Faye checked the clock and saw that it was time to wake up Lucy from her nap. She took her young daughter with her into the small kitchen where she finished getting dinner ready. She set Lucy on the kitchen floor with two of her favorite toys and filled a cup with fresh milk for her. Then she began cutting up potatoes, onions and carrots to put in with the pot roast which had been slow cooking on the stove since noon. Along with the pot roast she planned to put together her famous homemade biscuits, and when the meat was just done she would make beef gravy from the drippings. She had worked this morning on the Baklava they would have for dessert. Isaac was expected to bring a bottle of wine to toast the arrival of their cousins. The little twins, Aaron and Andre were still toddlers when she had seen them last at her wedding. She could hardly wait to see how they had grown.

Jacob returned home from work at 6:00 and smiled as he walked through the door and smelled the wonderful meal which was in preparation. This was truly his favorite part of the day. He paced wet kisses on the heads of little

Lucy and baby Emma who had just been woken up. Emma's dinner needed to be out of the way before the company came. Jacob gave Faye a playful wink as she left the room to nurse the baby. Then he took Lucy's hand and led her into the bedroom so she could help him get ready for the company.

Isaac and his family showed up at 6:45 with their cousin Alexander and little Andre in tow. Aaron would come next week with his Uncle Collins. The joy of the family reunion was dampened immediately by the look of anguish on Alex's face, and little Andre looked silently at the floor. "What's wrong?" Jacob asked. Apparently some bad news had reached them just before they left for dinner. "It's Collins and little Aaron. They got out of Turkey alright but there is a problem. Collins just wired us the news – the borders are closed. They were not allowed in the country." Faye walked up to them with baby Emma in her arms and little Lucy in tow. "What's this?" she asked. Her smile was soon replaced by shock and anguish. Who would have believed that their wonderful new country who had welcomed them with open arms would begin turning people away, and separate her young cousins. But thankfully, Alex and Andre were safe. They had made it to Seattle and there was still cause to celebrate. The table set, the food ready. Brother Isaac offered a prayer of thanksgiving over the meal.

"Lord God, we thank you for family and friends. We thank you for safe passage to Seattle for Alex and Andre. Take care of Collins and Aaron. Keep them and help them to find safe harbor. Now we give thanks for the meal my dear sister has prepared and pray your blessing upon this home. The families then began to dig into the delicious food and to enjoy the wine Isaac had brought. The dinner and visiting lasted until late into the evening, and even then good byes were hard to say. There were promises to see each other at the synagogue on Saturday, and an invitation to seder dinner on Friday night at Isaac's.

The company was now gone, the girls safely asleep in their beds. There was finally time for Jacob and Faye to talk together and to digest this news they had heard. "You were quiet tonight, my dear" Jacob said as they sat together on the worn sofa. Faye looked up into his face and her jaw trembled as she tried to control her emotion. "Jacob, what if that had been us? What if the borders had turned us away? I can't even imagine how Collins and Aaron must have felt not being allowed to enter the country. Can you imagine having the twins separated like that?" Jacob shook his head. "I know. I know. Alexander said that his brother was told that their vessel was heading to Canada and that there was possibly room for them there. We need to pray for them, and then release them to God's hands. He can keep them safe and show them where to go; what to do." They then went hand in hand into their bedroom, turning lights out as they went. Tomorrow would be a brand new day with new possibilities and promise. As for young Aaron, he and his Uncle Collins did find safe passage into Canada and settled in Montreal, Quebec. It wasn't until fifty years later that Andre and Aaron were able to find each other and re-connect. Both of their families were grown with grandchildren, and the entire family re-united to share in the happy time.

Depression Hits Hard

Life goes on, seasons change from fall to winter to spring. Life at the synagogue was busy, always a celebration in the Jewish community, a Bar mitzvah, or someone needing help. Jacob and Faye's family was growing as well with the birth of three more children. Albert arrived in 1925, David in June of 1927, and Thomas (Tommy) in 1929. The family was learning that another family of cousins were set to arrive in Seattle soon, as the Federal Government had decided to re-open the borders to immigrants. There was a chance that Jacob and Faye could take this family under their wing until they got established, as Brother Isaac had done for them. Faye sighed at the thought of the added responsibility. The year was 1931, and the entire country was in shock at the state of the countries economy and the recent collapse of the stock market. The world watched as the wealthy became penniless, and the lines of unemployed grew longer and longer. Seattle was hit hard by this as well. Jacob's once thriving shoe shine business at the successful Ben Paris Restaurant and Mercantile was really struggling. Jacob's customer base was mostly the successful business men. Bankers, investors, business owners, the leaders of the Seattle business community. These customers were the ones hit hardest by the market crash, and there was a ripple effect through the city. There were so many desperate people, so much need all around them. The good news is that Jacob's relationship with his employer at Ben Paris was solid, and he was able to work in the kitchen of the restaurant and bus tables, do dishes in the back – anything to help support this business and his family. The area churches and synagogues worked together to address the situation. It was family helping family, neighbor helping neighbor to meet the incredible need.

And now, the thought of them taking another family into their small home was almost overwhelming to Faye. Their budget was already stretched to maximum capacity. She smiled as she remembered the early years of their marriage and how Mama Romano had taught her to cook, making a wonderful meal out of inexpensive ingredients, almost making something out of nothing. A lot of love mixed with faith can do wonders. The memory of Jacob's mama warmed Faye's heart, and give her courage to face the daily challenges of raising a family of active children on a shoestring budget. Faye had just sent another letter to her London family to check in with them. They were busy with the daily running of their own business which was also affected by the global economy. No money or time for a visit to America to see their grandchildren. Ah, well, this was the risk they took when they embarked on this adventure to a new country and a new life. Faye had told her parents in her last letter that the children were thriving and very healthy. She did not, however, tell them about the child that was yet on the way. She had not even told Jacob yet. She felt a flutter in her heart at the very thought of a sixth child. She felt conflicted between excitement and overwhelming fatigue and sadness at the same time. As much as she loved her husband and her children she missed both sets of parents so much. Gone were the days where she could just sit and visit with them, share her heart and ask advice from them, and she felt the loss greatly. Faye sighed as she checked on two year old Tommy napping in the crib Jacob built for her just before Lucy was born. Five year old Davey was on the living room floor going between playing with his set of wooden blocks and looking at a picture book that her father had sent from England. Faye picked up a memory book she had made from pictures which commemorated their journey to America and the birth of their children. There were holiday and celebration times as her family grew – all memories never to be forgotten. She let soft tears fall onto the pages as she looked at the picture of her Jacob holding baby Lucy. Lucy was 12 years old now and growing into a lovely, respectful young woman. She was a smart girl, a good student, and a dutiful big sister to Emma age 10 and Albert age 7, making sure they got to school and home safely. She was also good at watching the children of others and was already baby sitting for families in the community.

Faye's tears continued to fall as she came to the part in her memory book which held letters she had received from her parents. She missed them so much! How could she have known when she left them to voyage across the sea that it would be so very long before she would see their sweet faces again. Just as Faye was about to be consumed by sadness a dear little voice brought her suddenly back to reality. She lifted her tear streaked face to see her little Davey looking intently into her sad eyes.

"Mama, what's wrong? Why are you crying? Why are you sad?"

Faye reached out her hand and caressed her young boy's face. "It's alright, darling. I was just looking at some old pictures of our family and letters from Grandma and Grandpa."

Davey's eyes lit up with excitement. "Can I see too?" he asked. Faye scooped up her son and set him on her lap, placing a tender kiss on the top of his head. "It's ok, honey. I'm not sad anymore. So, let's start from the beginning." With her son on her lap, Faye took him from the very beginning of their journey to America, through the birth of each of his siblings, and shared with him precious details about both sets of Grandparents and their life before they came to America.

Davey turned around and sat facing Mama. "What was it like, your life in Turkey? What did it look like there?" "Well;" Mama answered, "the land is beautiful. It's right on the seashore and there are great ships which come and bring food, wares, timber, lots of things from other countries. Life there was good. We were close to your grandparents and they helped us a lot. I know that they love you very much. It was hard to leave them and the land we had grown to love. But there were many years of war there." She held her son close to her breast. "Your father and I both decided that we did not want you exposed to that, that America would be a better place to raise our family.

Davey thought about this for some time. "Mama, do you miss it there?"

Faye had to fight hard against another wave of sorrow and tears. "I miss it very much, Son."

Davey, still deep in thought about all this, suddenly came up with an idea. "Mama, I know! When I am big, and a rich businessman, and when there is no more war, I will take you back there for a visit and you can show it to me."

"That sounds like a wonderful idea!" Faye exclaimed and held her son tight. She said a quiet prayer to God thanking him for this sweet, sensitive boy, and asking him for the opportunity someday to take this boy back to Constantinople for a visit and a glimpse back to her homeland and into her heart.

New Challenges Arise

The family was definitely growing. Soon after the birth of Baby Joey the cousins from the old country arrived. George and Francis along with little Mary and Florence became part of the family and Jacob helped George find employment at Ben Paris when work was available. By 1933 the nonstop activity around their small home continued to wear on Faye's nerves and she began to show signs of serious depression. Jacob worked so hard and did whatever he could to provide for his family and Faye would pick up extra jobs whenever she could. While others lost everything they had as the depression wore on, somehow her family was finding their way through it. The children continued to grow and were healthy and happy, learning by leaps and bounds. All, that is, but the baby. There was a nagging feeling and worry that something was very wrong with little Joey's development. Jacob tried to ease her fears. "Be patient with him, Fanny" he would say. "Each child develops at their own timing. I'm sure in time he will catch up with the others." Faye would feel better about it for a little while, but the nagging fears and uncertainties would always return. She finally decided that she needed to do something. Money or no money, she would take Joey to see the doctor tomorrow morning after the children left for school. Francis would be there at the house to watch over little Tommy and Florence while she was gone. That night after the children were in bed, Jacob and Faye had one of the biggest disagreements they had ever had.

"Faye, I do not know why you are doing this. Why you worry. How will we pay for this? I work and work and work and we never get ahead. This cursed depression will be the death of me. With all we need to deal with in this life, do we really need another problem?"

Faye answered through her tears "Jacob, I know. I know how hard you work and the pressures you are under. But I am a mother, and a mother knows when something is wrong with the child she loves. Please trust me on this, Jacob. I will find a way to help pay for this. This is our little baby, our youngest child. God help us – if there is something wrong with him we need to know." Jacob signed and paced about the room. Could something really be wrong with the baby? If there were health concerns it could really get expensive. Oh well, they had always found a way as a family, they could handle this as well. As they went to bed that night they both said prayers for their little boy, the one who had completely captured both their hearts. Tomorrow would be a big day for him. May God give the doctor wisdom to find anything wrong.

The next day Jacob hurried home from work to find the normal controlled chaos to be found in a household of four adults and eight children of varying ages. He looked into his wife's eyes as she and Frances put the finishing touches on their evening meal. Faye turned to her husband. "We'll talk later, dear. It'll be alright." She had a new confidence and resolution in her voice that he had not seen in a very long time. Whatever was going on with Joey, she was sure they could handle it. Dinner that night was full of chatter about school, friends and homework. At one interval in the conversation little four year old Tommy stood up on his chair with a scowl on his face and announced to everyone present that he would grow up to be a football player. This brought laughter and cheers all around the room. Faye stifled a laugh. "Alright, my little football player. Right now you need to sit back down and eat your food. You will need all your strength if you want to play football." Homework took the rest of the evening for the older ones and Florence, Tommy and Joey were in bed before sundown. When all homework was done and the house was quiet, Jacob and Faye had time together to work through the events of the day and the news that came with it. Jacob took her hands in his as they sat together on the sofa. "So, tell me how Joey did at the doctor. What did he say?"

Faye took a deep breath and gathered her strength to share the news she had been given. "Our baby will be just fine" she said. "But there is a problem with him. He can't hear." She looked into Jacob's eyes. "Jacob, Joey is deaf."

Jacob's world suddenly shifted and came to a screeching halt. His sweet baby – deaf? How could this be? How will he be able to learn? How can he have a future? "Fanny are they sure? Deaf? My poor little one! Did the doctor say anything else?"

Fanny actually had a look of peace on her face and a determined smile. "Jacob, like I said earlier, our baby will be fine. He's a smart boy. You and I can teach him. The children can help. Joey will have a life and a future. Sure it may be a little harder for him, but he is strong. He can learn. We can teach him how to read, and to read lips. As the children advance in their learning they can help teach him what they are learning. Really, Jacob, we can do this. It gives me new purpose and resolve as a mother. This little one will grow up to be as smart and as able as the other children."

Jacob was still working through the shock that came with this news. He shook his head as the gravity of this new reality hit him. "All right, my dear. We will teach him. We will get through this. With God's help we will find a way to do this." As they walked toward their bedroom they took a moment to stop by Joey's little bed. Jacob reached down and stroked his hair, putting a kiss on his forehead. Fanny was right. Joey would be fine. He had a hope and a future. With some hard work, lots of love and faith he would grow up strong, to be a good man of integrity. He would meet life's challenges and never give up. In the end, challenges which would come with this disability would only make him stronger.

God's Provision

Spring arrived within the little house on Capitol Hill in Seattle, and the family was abuzz with activity and excitement. Jacob's work at Ben Paris had picked up some with more clients returning to work. Tips were up slightly and that was a big help in making ends meet with the family budget. Jacob was continually amazed at his wife's ability to stretch their resources and provide healthy nutrition for the family on so little. She was definitely a smart, prudent wife. By now Cousin George and Francis had been able to find an apartment to rent. Francis was able to work for her company full time to help make ends meet. Faye still helped during the day sometimes with little Florence.

The children were excited about the upcoming summer break from school. They all had little jobs in the community to provide what they needed, and would work during the summer as well. Lucy and Emma had strong reputations as baby sitters and had a good sized list of parents they worked for. Faye would frown on the idea of them working on school nights, but opportunities would come for afternoons after school and some early evenings which would allow them to juggle work and homework. Albert had a job selling newspapers on the corner outside Ben Paris largest store. Even young David and Tommy would try selling magazines together door to door. Even though money was still tight in their city, the sight of these young boys, hand in hand, knocking on doors to make a little money was more than many could resist. They knew when Papa came home he would sit down with them and count their money, and figure out how much they made, dividing it between the two boys.

This morning breakfast was just winding up as Jacob came in from the bedroom and placed wet kisses on the heads of his children, blessing them for their day. Faye looked at him with apprehension – another morning with no breakfast? She followed Jacob to the front door and went outside with him, closing it behind her. "No breakfast again, Jacob?" She knew that many mornings when money was tight he would forgo breakfast to leave more food for the children.

"There will be eggs and toast at work for me" he responded. He kissed his wife on the cheek as he turned to walk towards the restaurant and set up his station. Faye's expression softened and a knowing smile came on her lips. The cook, of course! How many times had that sweet man fed her husband breakfast because he knew that they were struggling financially. She said a prayer of blessing on the man and then shouted after her husband "You tell cookie that there will be cake and pie for him after your next paycheck!" Jacob turned and waved, then set his mind to the day ahead, and the community that Jehovah God had called him to serve.

As Faye went back inside she saw that the children had cleared the breakfast dishes from the table, Joey was sitting content in his high chair and the children were collecting their schoolbooks and heading out for another busy day. She pulled David aside for a moment and placed a list inside his school book to be taken to the grocery store. "Son, I need you to take this list to the grocer on your way to school today. Tell him I will be by to pick up my order on Friday after Papa gets paid."

"Yes, Mama" David answered.

"Now David, I know how much you love the Halvah at the store, and how much you would like some this morning, but I'm afraid that the Halvah will have to wait. We will only have enough money for these groceries."

David looked at the floor and said, "yes, Mama." Faye's heart went out to the young boy. She hated having to pick and choose her groceries so carefully and not even having five cents for her boy who was delivering her list to the grocery store. "I'll tell you what" she said. "I just might have enough ingredients in the kitchen to make some Bischochos De Wevo cookies today for you children. Wouldn't that be a nice treat for after school today?"

David looked at Mama with a new light in his eyes. "Yes, Mama, that would be really neat!" Faye chuckled at her son as she patted his head. "Go now. You will need to hurry if you don't want to be late for school." David took off at a run in the direction of the corner grocery store, and Faye turned toward her kitchen to plan her day. There was Joseph to bathe and dress. He would busy himself on the kitchen floor with her pots and pans before it was time to put him down for a nap. The breakfast dishes were in the sink needing her attention. Before

Faye started her day she needed to do a little inventory. First she checked the coffee can in the kitchen cupboard which held the family's grocery money. She knew that it was empty yesterday, but was hoping against hope for a miracle. Empty again! Faye sighed and surveyed her kitchen. "Lord God of Abraham, Isaac and Jacob" she prayed "You know our situation. You know that we have no money and that there are doctor bills to pay for the baby, and that I just promised my son homemade cookies. I just ask you to supply to meet the need. Jacob works so hard to provide for us each day. Encourage his heart. Help the children with their school and their jobs. Amen." Faye felt encouraged and strengthened after her prayer and set herself to see exactly what she had on hand. She found some pieces of chicken in the freezer and took them out to thaw. In the refrigerator she found some milk and eggs. Funny, she didn't see them before! Then she turned to her cupboard and found flour, rice, beans and bullion cubes. There were enough ingredients for cookies for the children and a hearty stew for her family for supper. It also looked like there was enough flour and milk to make her favorite biscuits to go with the stew. There you go, she thought. We will be fine for today. God will be there to help us tomorrow, and we will be one day closer to Friday – Payday!

The children came home from school and rejoiced over the surprise of homemade cookies. David had kept their little secret like a champ and beamed when he saw the joy in his siblings faces at the treat Mama had prepared. The next morning Papa left for work early and Faye was agitated that the children were slower than usual with their breakfast. If they didn't eat faster they would be late for school. "What is this?" she asked them. "The clock does not stop while my children eat. Hurry now, finish your food. It's a new day with new possibilities." The children were quieter than usual and then they glanced at Lucy. She stood from her place and walked to where her mother stood. She reached into her pocket and put two dollars on the table, money she had been saving for shoes for school. She looked Mama in the eyes and said "Mama, we know that you and Papa are struggling. We know that there isn't enough food for Papa to eat breakfast." Emma stood and joined her sister. "here is my baby sitting money." She placed more money on the talble.

Faye looked in shock and embarrassment at the money her children were offering to help. Her girl's babysitting money – it was more than she could comprehend.

Albert was next. He looked a little embarrassed but stepped forward to offer his newspaper money. "This is a small house" he said, shifting from foot to foot. "We can hear you and Papa talking after we go to bed at night. Please, Mama. We want to help." David and Tommy were next, placing on the table a small box which held their magazine money. Emma then turned and grabbed Joey by the hand and helped him put a penny on top of the rest of the money – their combined offering. "Now" she said, "You go take this money we are giving, and pay the doctor bill. Then you take the rest to the grocery store and buy what we need."

Faye could no longer contain her emotion. "You dear, sweet, wonderful children! You are God's blessing to this home." She embraced the entire group and they all cried together, the children thankful to be able to help. "Now, off with you, you dears. You will be late today for sure!" The children ran to gather their books and out the door. Only Faye and Joey were left to gather up the pile of money the children left. Carefully, methodically, she counted the money at hand. Sure enough, there was enough money there to finish paying the doctors, stock up on what they needed, and set some aside for another day. Faye stopped short when she remembered the prayer she had prayed yesterday looking at the empty coffee can. Her eyes filled with tears once more as she realized that God had indeed sent his angels to provide their need. Six wonderful, precious angels named Lucy, Emma, Albert, David, Tommy and Joey!

Faye grabbed little Joey and put him on her hip, and took the money secured in David and Tommy's money box, She went first to the doctors office and paid their bill. Then she took her precious treasure to the corner store and stocked up on what they needed. There was enough for a celebration dinner that night and she even bought David's favorite – halvah for dessert.

The Best of Life

It was the later 1930's and the business scene of Capitol Hill and Downtown Seattle was beginning to change. There was an attitude of hopefulness on the streets instead that of great need and sadness. The city was beginning to heal from the ravages of the Great Depression. Jacob was given the opportunity to open more shoe shine businesses in Ben Paris' other shops in the Seattle area and Jacob constantly had his eyes open for honest and hard-working young men who just needed a break in their lives. He had never forgotten the stranger who had been his first customer, and later his good friend. This man had given him an opportunity when he was a stranger to the city with no job prospects and a pregnant wife to support. Jacob was driven to offer other young men the same opportunity that Jehovah God had brought his way.

The children were growing up so fast and Jacob was thankful that as his business grew he could now offer to his wife and children a few more of the comforts of life. Faye did such a great job of watching over the children, making sure that homework was done and also making sure their home was a welcoming place to come home to. Another opportunity with the new businesses was that Jacob and Faye were now able to approach the man they had been renting their home from about the possibility of buying it, which would bring his family another layer of security.

By the age of three, Joseph was finally learning to talk a little, though his speech was somewhat impaired by his hearing difficulties. Faye had discovered that if she held his face in her hands and spoke very clearly he could begin to repeat some of the words she was saying, and he would eventually begin to learn to read people's lips as he grew older. Faye determined that she would keep Joey home and teach him herself with the help of the older children, instead of sending him to school. With his severe hearing loss, the home would be the best environment for him to learn and move forward in life.

With the children growing older, Jacob and Faye could now enjoy more time at the synagogue they loved, Sephardic Bikur Holim on 52nd Avenue South in Seattle. Faye became very involved in the ladies auxiliary from this place of worship and her favorite time of the week was when the women of the ladies auxiliary gathered together at different homes to share recipes which were steeped in their culture and used to celebrate their special holidays. These recipes would eventually be compiled into a Sephardic cookbook, and be available for distribution from the synagogue. Jacob enjoyed spending time with the spiritual leaders he respected. By now Lucy and Emma were closely involved with youth activities at Bikur Holim and learning important lessons on carrying on the special traditions of their faith, preparing to have their own families someday. The boys were all involved in Hebrew school, learning to read from the Torah and understand God's law. The entire family enjoyed learning from the Torah each Saturday while attending services officiated by Rabbi Azose.

By mid-march, 1938, Faye turned her attention to what was always her favorite time of the year – the Passover. Such rich traditions, such great food, time to celebrate with family and to build family memories in the home and in the synagogue. It was so important to her to pass this history, faith and traditions on to her children, and to give them the opportunity to pass this gift of faith to her grandchildren someday. Faye intended to open her home to Jacob's brother Isaac and his family to celebrate the Passover in her home, and planned many special desserts and sweets to share with their friends and extended family at the Seder celebration at the synagogue. On her list to prepare was teslipishti (Passover cake), matzo balls, matzo meal pancakes and waffles, Passover mandel bread (like Biscotti), brownies and cookies. There was the remembrance meal with manor (bitter herbs), charoset (somewhat like granola), karpas (herbs), zeroah (shank bone of lamb), and beitzah (a dish made from beets). Faye knew the manor was her boy's least favorite part of the Seder meal, but it was really the most important part, as it helped the whole family to remember the bitterness of slavery in Egypt. The boys knew that the great feast of the Passover was coming with all their favorite foods to commemorate freedom from slavery and to remember their blessings, all God had done for them.

Faye had spoken to her sister-in-law, Elizabeth, and made plans for her to come over to their home a few days before the celebration began to help with the deep cleaning needed, putting away objects in the home not appropriate for such a solemn holiday, and with the cleaning and putting out of the candlesticks, special goblets for wine, head coverings, table cloths and mantle coverings important to the holiday. But for now and today, the important task was the planning to make sure that her cupboards were stocked with everything which would be needed for sharing the joy and importance of the Passover season with the rest of the family. There was plenty of time in the next few weeks to plan with Elizabeth, cook, bake, and work towards a Passover feast not soon to be forgotten.

Finally the day arrived. Jacob and Faye and the family returned home from the Synagogue dressed in their very best and anticipated the evening which was to come. Each child had a specific assignment each year, whether it was reading the story of the Exodus from the Torah, helping with the blessings over the candles and wine, or for the younger ones, answering questions to show they understood the history of the Jewish people and the importance of this holiday. Everyone was ready to observe the first night of this eight day observance. Four cups of wine would be poured, symbolizing the four stages that led the Hebrew slaves to their promise of freedom. These stages were: I will bring out, I will deliver, I will redeem, I will take. The fourth glass of wine is saved to the end of the celebration, sealing the Seder festivities.

During the meal, the passing of the matzah will also happen, another rich tradition of the Seder feast. The matzah is broken into three parts with the first piece eaten right away. The third piece is saved in a white cloth and set aside. The second piece can be used to keep the children focused or entertained during the celebration. Then after the feast, the third piece is eaten for dessert.

The time had now come to light the candles of remembrance with the traditional blessings over the candles. Faye rose from her place and knelt by little Joey, putting his face in her hands she said to him "Would you like Papa to pray over the candles now?" Joey's face broke into a contagious grin, and he said in his garbled speech "Wes, Papa, Pway". With this invitation, Jacob stood at his place and began the Hebrew blessing over the candles.

LEC HAH-OH-LAHM AH-SHER KEE-DEH-SHAH-NOO BEH-MITZ-VOH-TAHV VEH-TZEE-VAH VAN-NOO LEH-HAD-LEEK NER SHEL SHAH-BAHT KOH-DESH.

Blessed are you, Lord God, King of the universe, who has sanctified us with his commandments, and commanded us to kindle the light of the holy Shabbat.

BAH-ROOCH AH-TAH AH-DOH-NOI EH –LOH-HEH-NOO MEH-LECH HAH-OH-LAHM AH-SHER KEE-DEH-SHAH-NOO BEH-MITZ-VOH-TAHV VEH-TZEE-VAH VAN-NOO LEH-HAD-LEEK NER SHEL YOHM TOVH.

Blessed are you, Lord God, King of the universe, who has sanctified us with his commandments, and commanded us to kindle the Yom Tov light.

BAH-ROOCH AH-TAH AH-DOH-NOI EH –LOH-HEH-NOO MEH-LEC HAH-OH-LAHM SHEH-HEH-YAH-NOO VEH-KEE-YEH-MAH-NOO VEH-HEE-GHEE-AH-NOO LIZ-MAHN HAH-ZEH.

Blessed are you, Lord God, King of the universe, who has granted us life, sustained us, and enabled us to reach this occasion.

Long ago, at this season, on such a night as this, a people – our people – set out on a journey. All but crushed by their enslavement, they yet recalled the far off memory of a happier past. And heard the voice of their ancestral God, bidding them, summon up the courage to be free. Boldly, they went forth from Egypt, crossed the sea, and headed through the desert for the Promised Land. What they experienced, they remembered, and told their children, and they to theirs. From generation to generation, the story was retold, and we are here to tell it yet again. We too give thanks for Israel's liberation, we too remember what it means to be a slave. And we pray for all who are still fettered, still denied their human rights. Let all God's children sit at his table, drink the wine of deliverance, and eat the bread of freedom. Freedom from bondage. And freedom from oppression. Freedom from hunger. And freedom from want. Freedom from hatred. And freedom from fear. Freedom to think. And freedom to speak. Freedom to learn. And freedom to love. Freedom to hope. And freedom to rejoice. Soon in our days. Amen.

After the remembrance time of passing the manor, charoset, karpas, zeroah and beitzah – traditional Seder foods, the true feasting began. Faye and Elizabeth returned to the kitchen to get the kurabie, mandel bread, lamb with plenty of potatoes and gravy, borecas (eggplant turnovers), ponderikas (pretzel shaped bread sticks), and Passover pound cake and date bars for dessert. All foods the family loved and looked forward to. Jacob stood again to raise his glass to toast the healthy and happy family before him. He spoke the traditional Hebrew blessing over all children at the table. He was the happiest he had been in a very long time and watched with joy as the entire family, especially his sons, dug into the great feast the women had prepared. And as he listened to the light-hearted conversation and ate the mouth-watering food prepared for the feast, Jacob could not help but beam with pride at the scene before him. Yes, he thought, this indeed is the very best of life.

Waiting for News

It was spring of 1941 and war was raging in Europe. The terrors of Nazi Germany were ravaging the Jewish communities all over the region. Thankfully as there was a somewhat peaceful relationship between Turkey and Germany, the relatives in Istanbul were protected. The same was not true for Fanny's parents and sister in London, England. For the last nine months there had been bombing attacks on Britain by the Nazi Air Force, and Fanny had not heard from her family in a long time. She knew that mail from the bombing zone would be somewhat sporadic, still each day was a worry. Every day Faye lifted prayers to Jehovah God for their protection. Psalm 91 was her constant stay – "though thousands fall at your right hand it will not come near you."

The family was growing like crazy. Lucy, age 20, had met her soul mate Jack and there was talk of an upcoming wedding. She was working hard at a local clothing store and sharing a small apartment with 2 other girlfriends. Emma was 18 now and had left for California to go to college. Faye was thankful that Albert was too young at age 17 to be included in a military draft were one to take place – if the United States were to join the war effort in Europe.

David was as diligent with his schoolwork and after school job selling newspapers and magazines as 12 year old Tommy was with his football practices. Joey was 10 years old now and Faye continued to teach him at home, his brothers helping as well. Joey was excellent at reading lips by now and spoke well even though he had a minor speech impediment. Faye missed having her girls at home, but knew that this was their time to fly free and find their own way in life. She daily looked forward to the time her boys came home from school and work and she reveled in their youthful energy and antics. Every night when Jacob came home from Ben Paris she would look at him with pleading eyes. "Has there been any mail?" she would ask. He would look at her sadly and say, "No, my love. There was no letter from London today." Faye would sigh and send another prayer to heaven for her family.

David kept her updated on the news from Europe, supplying her with a newspaper when new information came out. From the newspapers Faye learned that the residents of London were able to take refuge in the subway tunnels which the city opened up to shelter them from the nightly bomb attacks. This gave her some reassurance that her family would survive even this.

But along with this reassuring news of London was also daily news of the atrocities that the Jewish people were facing at Auschwitz and other Nazi death camps. These were God's chosen people – her people, and it literally broke her heart. Each evening after Supper the family held a somber time of prayer for the situation in Europe before the boys began their homework that evening.

Then one day Jacob came home from work with a new light in his eyes. Faye looked up from her dinner preparations and there, in his breast pocket was a letter. "Jacob, " she said, "Is this the word we have been waiting for? Is that letter from my family?" His smile was all she needed as an answer. He reached into his pocket and handed her the letter. Than he took her by the hand, and led her to the sofa where they could read the letter together. She opened the letter and saw that it was dated February, 1941. They had survived the most intense phase of the attack. Mother wrote that they were indeed spending their nights in the underground subways and that this was keeping them safe. The building their business was run out of was hit by the bombing attack early on, but they were already planning to rebuild and move forward. They were growing closer to each other as a family and growing closer to God, gaining strength from their faith.

"They are ok. They have survived even this. God be praised!" Faye wiped tears from her eyes and felt relief flood through her being. She knew that her family rested safe in God's hands. She knew that they all did. Her precious children would grow up and follow God's plan for their lives. All was well.

December 7, 1941

David was convinced in his heart that he would never forget today. This day would completely change and define the country he loved with all his soul. This country which had welcomed his parents with open arms, and helped them to become established. Nothing would be the same for a very long time, and his neighborhood was beginning to react with shock and disbelief.

Papa was at work, Mama and Joey were at home, Albert was still at high school finishing up his last class of the day, and Tommy had already left school for football practice. Even though their football season was over, a group of boys still gathered three times a week to exercise and work on their skills. 15 year old David had scheduled earlier classes to accommodate his daily paper and magazine sales job on the corner by his Dad's business. Now, looking at the huge stack of special bulletins just put out from the Associated Press and freshly printed, he was glad he had arranged his class schedule around his job.

"Extra, extra – special bulletin from the Associated Press. There has been a Japanese air raid upon the U.S. Navy at Pearl Harbor. Thousands of sailors lost. Read all about it!"

David was sure that Papa had heard word of the attack,

but not sure if Mama and Joey at home had heard. His stack of bulletins was diminishing when he saw 12 year old Tommy walking towards him on his way home from practice. "Tommy, take this paper home and show it to Mama. Tell her to turn on the radio. I won't be home until late. I am needed here. The guys will be here soon with a fresh stack of bulletins." David's voice broke from emotion. "Tell Mama I love her!" Tommy took one look at the bulletin then broke into a run toward home.

David took just a minute to re-read the bulletin which had greeted him when he had arrived at his job. "WASHINGTON – December 7, Associated Press – President Roosevelt said in a statement today that the Japanese had attacked Pearl Harbor, Hawaii, from the air. The President is ordering the Army and Navy to carry out undisclosed orders prepared for the defense of the United States."

Jacob closed his shoe shine shop at Ben Paris' restaurant and store as soon as the line of customers cleared out. After he heard the news of the attack on Pearl Harbor he had only one thing on his mind – his Faye. He needed to get home to Fanny. Jacob sent quick word to Cookie in the kitchen that his David was still on the nearby street corner handing out bulletins. Cookie quickly put together a basket of food for him for supper. Jacob stopped for a moment to check on him and bring him his supper. David hugged his father, thankful for the food and encouragement. "Thanks for the food. I will be here for a while yet. Go home and tell Mana that I will be home when I can."

When Jacob arrived home Faye, Albert, Tommy and

Joey were gathered around the radio. He placed kisses on the heads of his children, and then went to Faye, pulling her to her feet and into his arms. She still held in her hand the Bulletin that Tommy had brought home to her. Her face was white as a sheet and there was a look of terror in her eyes. Jacob looked to his children and said, "You keep listening to the news. David will come home when he can. Mama and I need to talk." The children nodded at him and turned their attention back to the radio.

Jacob and Faye entered into their bedroom and shut the door behind them. In the privacy of their bedroom the reality of the situation and what it meant for their country could be discussed. Faye turned to her husband. "David – you saw him? He is alright?" Jacob nodded. "Yes. He wanted to stay at his post and pass out the rest of the bulletins. Cookie heard and sent him some supper. He's a good boy – He wanted to do something to help."

Faye nodded. Then the tears started to come and again Jacob pulled her into a hug. "They are talking about war. I hate war! We came here to America to escape war. Whatever will we do?" Jacob said "I know. I know. We need to pray. We cannot stand by and just watch while our country is being attacked. We must fight back." Faye shook her head. "But Jacob, it won't be us fighting back – it will be our children. **Our** children, Jacob!" Again, Jacob nodded. He understood. As a young man he had chosen to fight for what he believed in. Now his sons had the same choice before them. All Jacob knew was that his world had changed forever. Nothing would ever be the same again. David made it home late that night, completely exhausted but extremely proud of the part he played in warning his community of what had happened and what was to come. No homework for him tonight. He quickly dressed into his pajamas and crawled into his bed. Mama would write a note about the homework, his teachers would understand.

The next day found the family again gathered around the radio listening to President Roosevelt's address to the nation. "Mr. Vice President, Mr. Speaker, Members of the Senate and of the House of Representatives: Yesterday, December 7th, 1941 – a date which will live in infamy – the United States of America was suddenly and deliberately attacked by Naval and Air Forces from the Empire of Japan. The attack yesterday on the Hawaiian Islands has caused severe damage to American Naval and Military forces. I regret to tell you that very many Americans have been lost. In addition, American ships have been reported torpedoed on the high seas between San Francisco and Honolulu. Japan has therefore undertaken a surprise offensive extending through the Pacific area. … The facts of yesterday and today speak for themselves. The people of the United States have already formed their opinions and well understand the implications to the very life and safety of our nation."

So that was that. The United States of America was now at war, and because of the acts of the day before had joined the war efforts which Europe was already involved in. The family sat quietly after the radio address was over and let the reality set in. Newlywed Lucy stood up first, took her husband Jack's hand and pulled him to his feet. "We had a long talk last night. Jack wants to enlist in the Army and help with the Military Offensive."

Faye nodded, sad but so very proud. "Emma called last night from California. Gene and Emma have been talking about getting married. Gene decided last night to enlist as well. Emma will wait for him here at home, and they will be married when he returns. By now there were tears in everyone's eyes. Yes, things would change, but the love within this family would stay strong. Seventeen year old Albert stood to his feet, resolute at what he knew he needed to do. "Mama, Papa, I will be eighteen years old in three months. I want to test out of High School and graduate early, then I want to enlist in the Army as well. I have to help too. We can't let them attack us like that."

Jacob looked at his growing family – so proud of the young people they were becoming. He stood and offered to lead his precious family in prayer to God. "O Lord our God, Great Jehovah, we pray that you watch over our country. Grieve with those who now grieve having lost husbands and sons. Be with the wounded and bind up their wounds. Comfort and encourage their families. And most of all, O Lord our God, watch over these children of ours. We thank you for their brave hearts and their willingness to help our Country at this perilous time. Bless and protect them, and bring them home safe and sound. No father could be prouder than I am right now."

David wanted to help as well, but knew he was still too young. If he had his way he would enlist into the Navy. Not as a sailor, but as an officer. He wanted to sign up for college courses to make this happen. Some day he would do his part as an officer sailing on a Naval Ship and fight for the freedom of the land he loved.

The Homecoming

Twenty year old David Romano adjusted the rudder on the Naval sail frigate he was using as part of his Naval Fire Officer position located in Newport, Rhode Island. The Department of the Navy allowed their Officers to take sail boats out onto the waters by the training facility to work on their sailing skills and to keep the boats in good working order. World War II had been over for almost a year now. There was a large number of men enlisted and drafted into the war and it took time to process discharge papers. As David was a newer recruit he had to wait his turn to be discharged. He was encouraged to stay on at the training facility in Rhode Island and continue with his basic training exercises. When he was able he always looked forward to working on his sailing skills off Narragansett Bay. He let out his sail on the boat to catch any wind the August afternoon would bring him. He had time to think, to relax and remember all that had happened since the United States had joined Europe in the war.

David had stayed the course set before him and enlisted, offering first to take Naval Officer training courses at Gonzaga University in Spokane, Washington. Then he left for basic training in Rhode Island and what do you know…when he reached his destination he found out that the war was over. As much as he was willing to defend his country, he was grateful he could do so without fighting in any battles. His thoughts went to the family he left behind in Seattle. Thankfully his brother and brothers in law had all escaped serious injury and returned home by now. Lucy and Jack were expecting their first child. Emma and Gene were married in the Seattle area as soon as he was discharged, then returned to California to finish their college education. Albert had returned home to marry Marilyn, his high school sweetheart. Tommy had been offered a full ride scholarship to Stanford University to play the position of defensive linebacker on their football team. He would leave for college next week with his girlfriend, Collette, so he could begin practicing with the team. Young Joey was now fourteen years old. He still had a speech impediment because of his hearing loss, but the whole community knew and loved him as a bright young man with a heart of gold. Here, David thought, sailing on waters off Newport Beach and finishing his basic training, life was certainly good. He truly believed that the young men he trained with would become valuable friends for many years to come.

Word finally came to David from the Department of the Navy in October of 1946 that his discharge papers finally were processed, and his days of service to the Navy were soon to be over. A few Navy buddies also being discharged were from the Miami Beach area and were planning to rent an apartment together, and they invited David to join them for a while before he made his way back to Seattle, to which he heartily agreed. The

Navy would give them vouchers for a free airline ticket to anywhere in the United States. So the plan was to head to Miami Beach with his friends and spend the winter there. He would look for a job there so he could earn money for his eventual airline ticket home. In the meantime it would be sunshine, the beach, his buddies, and girls.

A few days after they arrived he went to the pay telephone at the corner store to call home and check in. The news he heard from Mama stopped his world short. "David, please come home right away. Your papa was diagnosed last month with an aggressive lung cancer. His health has been deteriorating so very fast. We have been trying to get word to you. Please hurry home. He doesn't have long to live." "Mama, I will be there as soon as I can. Tell Papa that I love him and that I am on my way." He felt hot tears fill his eyes as he hung up the telephone, but would not let himself give into them. He had to find a way to get home and fast. He stopped quickly by the apartment to let the guys know that his father was dying and that he needed to fly home right away. His friends pooled their money together to try to help him get home but it was not near enough money to purchase a ticket home. David had no choice. Even though his travel documents were already stamped, he would have to try to use them again. On a wing and a prayer he quickly packed his bags and hailed a cab to take him to the airport.

Upon his arrival there he saw a large crowd of uniformed service men with their travel vouchers being processed for a plane ride home. David stayed with these service men and continued through the line toward the ticketing agents, trying his best to stay calm and act natural. When he finally reached the ticket counter the Agent seemed distracted by a conversation he was having with the agent next to him. He did not notice that David's voucher had already been stamped and the man gave him a pass for a flight to Los Angeles International Airport, then a transfer flight to the Seattle area. He felt relieved as he realized he would be more than half way home. As he made his way to his seat on the plane he said a silent prayer that God would help his father to hang on until he got home. He was so worried about him and about his mother. He wondered how she was holding up under these circumstances. "Please, God, help me" he prayed. "I need to get home". The flight went late into the night and early the next morning he landed in Los Angeles. David disembarked the plane and followed the posted signs for Military personnel on their way home. To his dismay, he saw that the ticket counter for Military flights was nearly empty so chance of distraction here was small. He started to sweat and his hands began to become clammy. What if he was caught? He could easily do jail time and never see Papa again.

He took a deep breath and stepped up to the ticket counter, transfer pass to Seattle in his hand. The ticket agent was all business. "I need to see your initial ticket voucher as well" he said. David flashed him a quick smile and pulled the voucher out of his pocket, handing it to the Agent. "I'll be just a minute" he said, stepping away from the ticket counter. The man returned with an Army Staff Sargent in tow. "Son," the man said, "you will need to come with me." "Now I've really done it!" he thought. "I will do time in the brig for sure!" The stern Army Sargent led him to a side room and sat him down. "Your voucher has already been stamped, Sailor! What do you have to say for yourself? Are you taking advantage of the Navy's good graces in giving you a free flight home?"

David looked at the floor, his shoulders slumped in defeat. Finally two tears escaped his resolve and made their way down his face. "No, no Sir" he said quietly. "Speak up, Sailor. Tell me why you did this." David took a deep breath and knew it was time to come clean and tell the Sargent the truth. "Aw, I'm sorry, Sir. I planned to spend the winter on Miami Beach with some of my Navy brothers, and find a job to pay my way home to Seattle in the spring. But when I called home to check in with my mother she told me that my father is dying from lung cancer. He is really sick and doesn't have long to live. I didn't have time to wait until I could earn enough money to fly home." He looked at the floor again, praying for courage to stay strong and continue with his story. "I showed my voucher to the agent at the airport in Miami, but here were so many military guys there with their vouchers the agent didn't notice that mine was already stamped. They processed the voucher a second time and gave me a transfer pass to get me to Seattle." Finally he stood to his feet for his final appeal. "Please Sir, Please. I need to get home. My father won't last much longer!"

The Sargent looked at him with a little more compassion now. "Alright, sailor. Sit back down here and wait for me. I will be back after I check out your story." David sat again on the bench provided for him and wrote down the telephone number for the Sargent to call. Then he waited. And he waited. And he waited. This was definitely the longest twenty minutes of his young life. Finally the Sargent returned. "Your story checked out" he said in his strictest Staff Sargent voice. Then the man relaxed and held out his hand in which he had a new voucher for a trip home to Seattle. "Go home, Son. See your father before he dies. He doesn't have much time left." David exhaled, relieved beyond words. He smiled and vigorously shook the man's hand. "Yes sir. Thank you, sir!" He took his voucher and jogged toward the ticket counter, all the while praying he could get home in time.

Jacob had been sent home from the hospital to die peacefully surrounded by the family he spent his life loving and serving. Everyone was gathered there to say their good byes, all except David. When his flight landed in Seattle David disembarked the plane and ran through the airport as fast as he could run. He hailed a cab and gave the man his home address. "Please sir, my father is dying. I need to get home as fast as I can." This was all that the cabby needed to hear. He literally flew through the city streets toward Capitol Hill. When they finally arrived home he thanked the man and asked him how much he owed for the ride. The cabby said "There's no charge on this trip. Thank you for your service, son. Go see your father". David had forgotten in the emotion of the moment that he was still dressed in his Navy uniform. "Yes sir. Thank you sir." He exited the taxi and jogged up the walkway to the front porch of the house and in the front door.

Faye was the first to see him and ran up to her son, engulfing him in a long hug. Now David could no longer contain his emotions and the tears took over. He just held his precious, sweet mama in his arms and let the moment sink in. At last he found some composure and pulled back. "How is he doing?" She gave him a half smile and said "Come and see for yourself". He followed her into the bedroom and saw all his siblings standing around their parent's bed. When they saw him there were gasps and squeals of excitement. He was suddenly surrounded by his wonderful family all showering him with hugs and kisses. He could not believe how good it felt to be home – even under these circumstances. Jacob was sleeping in his bed, his breathing a bit labored. Faye went over to the bed and spoke to her husband. "Jacob, wake up dear. David has come home, Jacob." David walked over and knelt by the bed. "That's right, Papa. I'm here to see you. Wake up, Papa." Slowly Jacob opened his eyes and looked at his son. "Is this really my brave sailor?" "Yes, Papa, It's me!" David said. Jacob said "Come sit by me and tell me all about your adventures." David sat on the edge of his bed and looked into his Papa's eyes. Age had made them a bit dimmer but the light of God and life was still there. He told his sweet Papa about his experiences in Rhode Island, his basic training and afternoons sailing in the Navy sailboats. About the good people he had met and the friendships he had made. After a while David stood and said, "Papa, we can talk more later. You sleep some more." Jacob nodded and closed his eyes. Lucy said "Mama has been expecting you, David. She made enough food for supper to feed the entire Navy. Come and she will prepare you a plate." David kissed his Father on the forehead and followed his siblings out into the living area. There he sat in Papa's favorite chair and caught up with his siblings and their spouses while Mama brought him an enormous plate of his favorite foods.

That was the last conversation David had with Papa. It wasn't long before Jacob's breathing became more labored and he lost consciousness. By two o'clock the next morning he was gone, safe in Abraham's bosom. Faye proved to be the strong Jewish woman she had been all her life, doting on her children while missing her husband desperately. Her Jehovah God would give her strength and purpose, courage to live on. She had an amazing family and community to lean on for support. They had a funeral service at the Synagogue and the facility was filled to capacity, not only by the Jewish community but also by the business community he served at the Ben Paris' Restaurant and Store. Ben Paris himself was in attendance and of course, wonderful, faithful Cookie. They all gathered afterwards at the graveside where they laid Faye's precious Jacob to rest. Even though the good bye was heartbreaking, she knew her precious husband was free from pain and from the ravages of the cancer. Faye looked around at the group of wonderful friends and family. "Yes, Lord God. Look at this great crowd of people who love us. I will continue to serve You, our community and Your synagogue. I will be just fine."

As for David, it was time for him to go on with his life and find what God had put him here on earth to do. He thought he might start by checking with the company he had sold magazines for while he was a teenager. Maybe they would have an open position. And do you know what? They did, and this job opening grew into a career that would last him all his working life. And it wasn't too long after he returned to Seattle that on the shores of Lake Washington he met a beautiful girl named Beverly who would soon become the love of his life, and eventually my mother. Thus began a love that would reach beyond fifty nine years. But that, of course, is another story entirely.

Left to right in this photo are Lucy, Emma,
Jacob, Joey, Tommy, Faye, David and Albert

Printed in the United States
By Bookmasters